SUGAR
~ on ~
SNOW

Nan Parson Rossiter

DAVID R. GODINE · *Publisher*

Boston

Published in 2011 by
DAVID R. GODINE · *Publisher*
Post Office Box 450
Jaffrey, New Hampshire 03452
www.godine.com

Library of Congress Cataloging-in-Publication Data

Rossiter, Nan Parson.
Sugar on snow / Nan Parson Rossiter.
p. cm.
Summary: Brothers Ethan and Seth spend a long day
helping their parents gather sap and make maple syrup
when March brings the first hint of spring to their New England farm. Includes a legend of how Native Americans first
began to make and use maple syrup.
ISBN 978-1-56792-370-4 (softcover)
[1. Maple syrup—Fiction. 2. Family life—New England—
Fiction. 3. Brothers—Fiction. 4. New England—Fiction.] I.
Title.
PZ7.R72223Su2015
[Fic]—dc22
2010043534

Design by Beth Herzog

SECOND SOFTCOVER PRINTING, 2015
Printed in Canada

For Cole and Noah, my heart's delight!
And for my "other" mom and dad, Peter and Gaila Rossiter

The mountains and the hills shall break forth into singing…
And all the trees of the field shall clap their hands.

ISAIAH 55:12

Seth and Ethan raced back to the house after finishing their chores. The March evening was chilly, but the wind didn't have the icy sting of winter. For the first time that year, it carried just a hint of spring. Seth reached the door first and burst into the kitchen, his younger brother right behind him.

"Mom!" yelled Seth. "The sap's really running. Tomorrow's the day!"

"Do you think so, too, Mom?" asked Ethan. "Will we make syrup tomorrow?"

"Looks like we might," Mom answered as she set the table for dinner. "The buckets were pretty full when your dad and I did a gathering run this morning. If this weather holds, we'll do another one tomorrow and start boiling."

"I've grown a lot since last spring," said Ethan, straightening up to his full height. "I bet I'll be able to help with the buckets this year."

"Me, too," said Seth quickly. "And I can help drive the tractor. Can't I?"

"We'll see," Mom answered. "But there will be lots to help with—including the tasting."

The boys grinned at each other, and Mom laughed.

"Go wash up for dinner. If you're going to help with anything, you need to keep up your strength."

They were almost too excited to eat. Ethan finished first and went to the window to peer out at the distant maple trees.

For once, the boys didn't need to be reminded to go to bed on time. "We'll have to get up early tomorrow," Seth said. "Anyway, the sooner we fall asleep, the sooner it'll be morning."

He lay in bed listening to Ethan's soft breathing. Morning seemed very far away. He had waited so long to be old enough to steer the tractor. *Please let tomorrow be the day*, he wished, squeezing his eyes shut and crossing his fingers.

The dawn sky was just beginning to brighten when Seth heard tapping at the bedroom door.

"Wake up, boys," Mom called softly. "Today's the day. Ready to go get some sap?"

"Ethan, get up!" Seth whispered excitedly. He climbed down from the top bunk and threw a pillow at his brother, who was still sleepily rubbing his eyes. "Hurry up! We're sugaring off today!"

Outside the window, the melting snow dripped rhythmically. The boys pulled on jeans and sweaters and bumped down the stairs to find Mom in the kitchen filling thermoses with coffee and hot chocolate. She spooned steaming oatmeal into bowls.

"Where's Dad?" Seth asked.

"He's getting the tractor ready."

"Let's go!" said Ethan. He and Seth headed toward the mudroom door.

"Whoa! Food first," reminded Mom. "There'll be plenty of work waiting for us after breakfast." The boys ate so fast that they barely tasted the food. As soon as they were done, they bolted for their jackets and boots and ran outside.

By the time Mom had added wood to the kitchen stove, let out Maple the cat, and packed the lunch basket, the boys had already reached the sugarhouse. The old green and yellow tractor rumbled and hummed nearby. Dad checked the big metal holding tank strapped onto the trailer behind it.

"Here comes my crew!" he called when he saw the boys. "Who's riding with me?" Ethan looked eagerly at Dad, then at Seth.

"Come on, guys, there's room for both of you." Seth and Ethan both gave a hoot of joy and scrambled up onto Dad's lap.

"Everybody ready?" Dad called.

"Ready!"

The family's black Lab, Chloe, barked and raced around excitedly as Dad put the tractor in gear and headed for the sugar bush, a big grove of maple trees about a quarter of a mile across the field. Mom followed close behind in the path cut through the snow by the tractor. "Look!" she called, pointing to a tree branch overhead. "The first robin of the season!"

When they reached the road that ran through the sugar bush, Dad slowed the tractor to a crawl and lifted Ethan down. "What do you think, Seth?" Dad asked. "Are you ready to steer?"

"Yes!" cried Seth. He paid close attention as Dad showed him how to work the gears.

Seth grinned as he settled into the high tractor seat. The whole world looked different from up there, and he loved the way the engine rumbled quietly under him.

At least one metal bucket hung from every sugar maple in the grove. "When did you tap the trees, Dad?" asked Seth, keeping his eyes on the road.

"Three days ago, after we had those two warm days in a row. Nice days like that with freezing-cold nights in between are just what maples need to get their sap rising," answered Dad.

"Why do we always say 'sap's rising,' when it's really dripping down out of the tree?" asked Ethan.

"The warm weather wakes up the sap in the tree's roots and makes it rise up to the branches," explained Dad, as they walked alongside the tractor. "Then when it's cold at night, it seeps back to the roots."

"This bucket's full," called Mom. "Here it comes!"

Mom poured the contents into the holding tank. Dad was next, emptying his bucket from the other side of the trailer. He took both empty buckets and turned back toward the tree to hang them up again. "I can do that!" cried Ethan. He took the buckets from Dad and rehung each one from a spout, carefully covering them with their peaked metal lids.

"Nice job, Ethan," said Dad. "That'll save a lot of time." Filling the tank was slow work, since most trees were well off the road.

Seth stopped and started the tractor often. When he reached the end of a row, he climbed down to help with the buckets while Dad guided the tractor to the next section of trees.

Little by little, the sap level in the tank began to rise. "It's more than half full," Dad said finally, peering into the tank. "How about a lunch break?"

"I'm starving," said Seth.

"Me, too," said Ethan. "I wish we had some syrup right now."

"We'll have to wait a while for syrup," said Mom. "Let's see if we can get by on sandwiches."

The sandwiches and hot chocolate were gone in a flash. "Another five minutes," said Dad, "and it's back to work."

"I'm going to get the fire started in the sugarhouse," said Mom. "Do you boys want to come watch, or stay and help empty buckets?"

"Stay and help!" said Ethan and Seth together.

"Okay," said Mom. "See you soon."

Seth turned off the tractor and climbed down beside the trailer. The snow crunched under his feet. "I can bring the buckets over," he suggested. "Especially the ones that aren't so full."

"Let me empty them!" called Ethan.

"We'll give it a try," Dad said.

Seth chose a bucket and handed it up to his brother. Ethan slowly tipped the bucket and poured the sap into the tank.

"And I can hang it back up," said Seth, taking the empty bucket from Ethan.

"You're quite a team!" said Dad. "We'll have a full tank of sap ready to boil before you know it."

By the time the sap run was finished, the sun was low in the sky, and a light snow was falling. Chloe led the way, though she looked weary from a busy day of chasing rabbits and squirrels. "I know how she feels," said Seth as the tractor chugged toward home. He knew that someday he would be the one to steer the tractor to and from the sugar bush, but tonight he was perfectly happy to leave the driving to Dad.

From the top of the open field, they could see the glow of the sugarhouse ahead. When they reached it, Dad stopped the tractor, and the boys hopped down. "We did it, guys!" Dad said. "Gimme five!"

Ethan and Seth laughed and smacked Dad's hand.

"I'm going to start boiling the sap," said Dad. "Why don't you two go inside and help your mother with supper?"

This time, Ethan and Seth made no move to follow him. They were both hungry, and their arms ached from lifting the heavy buckets.

The soup and grilled-cheese sandwiches were delicious. While the boys finished eating, Mom fixed an extra plate for Dad.

"You two look tired," she said. "Are you sure you want to come?"

"Of course we want to!" said Seth.

"Yeah," said Ethan. "The sugarhouse is the best part."

"Go ahead, then," said Mom. "You can take the food to Dad. I'll be down in a while."

The boys pulled on their jackets and stepped outside into the snowy night. Huge billows of steam rose from the sugarhouse, filling the air with the thick, sweet smell of maple mixed with wood smoke.

Inside, Dad was busy measuring the temperature of the sap boiling in the big evaporator pans.

"That's a lot of sap," said Ethan, peering down into the swirling golden liquid.

"It takes a lot of sap to make a little syrup," said Dad. "Sap is mostly water, you know. Syrup is what's left after most of the water boils off. Forty gallons of sap make only one gallon of maple syrup!"

Before stopping to eat supper, Dad strained the last bucket of sap so that no stray leaves or twigs would get into the boiler.

Ethan and Seth took turns skimming the foam off the syrup until Mom opened the door, letting in a little gust of snow. She had a thermos of coffee tucked under her arm, since she and Dad would be up most of the night tending the syrup. She also had a plate of doughnuts, a jar of pickles, and two empty bowls. Seth stood up. He knew what the bowls were for.

"Is it time yet, Dad?"

"I think it's just about ready," Dad answered. "Go ahead."

"Come on, Ethan!" Seth said. The boys ran outside and packed the bowls with snow. Then they dashed back into the sugarhouse and handed the bowls to Dad.

"Thanks for your help today, guys," he said, smiling. "You've certainly earned this," he added as he took a long spoon and drizzled syrup over the mounds of snow. The hot syrup was golden and clear, and it turned gooey as it hit the snow. Seth and Ethan scooped big bites into their mouths.

All the sweetness of the day melted on their tongues.

Afterword

Legend has it that, on an early spring day while there was still snow on the ground, a Native American chief struck a tree with his ax but was called away to do something else before he could finish chopping it down. No one noticed that a clear liquid began to drip from the gash in the bark.

Earlier that day, the chief's wife had left a wooden bowl at the base of the tree, and gradually the bowl began to fill with the watery substance. When the chief's wife was ready to start the evening meal, she picked up the bowl and was surprised to see that it was already full of water. She poured it over the meat she had prepared and let it simmer for several hours. That evening, her family repeatedly complimented her cooking. They all wanted to know what she had done differently. The chief's wife was puzzled, because she hadn't changed her recipe one bit. It was not until the next day that she noticed the clear substance dripping from the tree and realized that she had cooked not with water but with tree sap! Out of curiosity, women in the tribe tried cooking the sap of other trees, but discovered that it was only the sap of the maple that cooked down into such a flavorful substance.

The gathering and distilling of maple sap has changed considerably since Native Americans first began to use it in their cooking. For many decades people in the northeastern United States and parts of Canada hammered wooden taps into the trees and collected the sap in buckets, like those shown in this book. Some farms still do it this way, but most consider the method time-consuming and old-fashioned. Modern farms use plastic tubing that runs from tree to tree and carries the sap directly to the sugarhouse. The tubing is not nearly as picturesque as the buckets hanging from the trees, but it certainly simplifies the job of making maple syrup.

There's one New England tradition that remains unchanged, however—when enjoying sugar on snow, don't forget the homemade doughnuts and sour pickles!